CD ROM
inside
back cover.

DAWUD WHARNSBY

A Picnic of Poems In Allah's Green Garden

ILLUSTRATED BY

SHIREEN ADAMS

THE ISLAMIC FOUNDATION

Published by
THE ISLAMIC FOUNDATION

Distributed by
KUBE PUBLISHING LTD.
Markfield Conference Centre
Ratby Lane, Markfield,
Leicestershire, LE67 9SY
United Kingdom
Tel: +44 (0) 1530 249230
Fax: +44 (0) 1530 249656
Email: info@kubepublishing.com
Website: www.kubepublishing.com

Poems, prose and song lyrics are all
published with the permission of the author.

A Catalogue-in-Publication Data record for
this book is available from the British Library.

ISBN: 978-0-86037-444-2

Author Dawud Wharnsby
Illustrator Shireen Adams
Editor Haris Ahmad
Production Manager Anwar Cara
Cover/Book Design & typeset Nasir Cadir

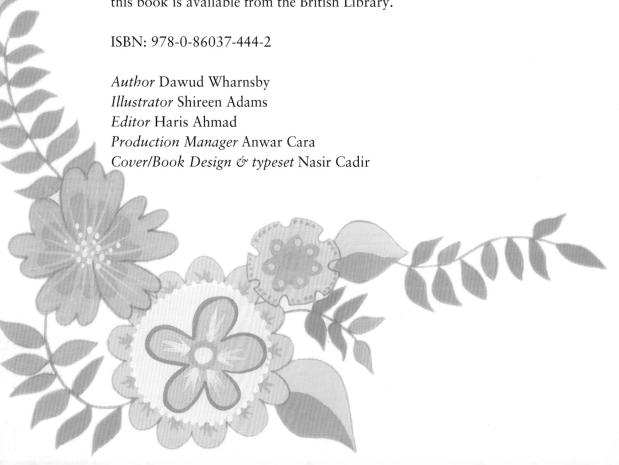

A Picnic of Poems

I've packed some poems for lunch,
some rhymes for us to chew,
a simple, sippy, soup of songs,
to stir and sing and stew.

Like all good meals to munch,
it would be very rude,
not to begin with *bismillah*,
to bless our poetry food.

Lorry, Cycle and Feet

Lorry! Lorry!
Drivin' down the road.
Bangin', clingin' and clangin'
and carryin' such a load.
So heavy strong and high,
as you go bouncing by.
Lorry! Lorry!
Drivin' down the road.

Cycle! Cycle!
Spinnin' down the street.
Whirrin' with wheels a purrin',
under one old comfy seat.
So shiny in the sun,
you've only room for one.
Cycle! Cycle!
Spinnin' down the street.

My feet! My feet!
Walking everywhere.
Trippin', runnin' and skippin'.
and takin' me here and there.
I ask *Allah* each day,
to help me on my way.
My feet! My feet!
Walking everywhere.

Storm

I love when a storm,
sings down from the sky,
and drums upon the streets.

It rains its rhythms,
upon my rooftop,
while I'm beneath my sheets.

I love when the wind,
is wild and whistles,
through leaves of waving trees.
My bed like a boat,
in a storm afloat,
dreaming upon high seas.

Rose

I wonder if a thorny twig even knows,
that one day it will blossom and will grow a lovely rose.

I wonder of my own life, what is it I'll be?
The twiggy little stick I am – will I become a tree?

Roots so deep and strong, my arms up to the sky?
Bring cool shade, sweet fruits and flowers to those who
pass me by?

God gives us choices to grow in better ways.
Our best is yet to come, as long as we wake to new days.

So, though today I'm small, there will come an hour.
Tomorrow may be my day, to blossom, bloom and flower.

If it's meant to be, and God wills it for me,
I will beautify this world, like a rose bush or fruit tree.

Just be patient with me, we'll wait and see.

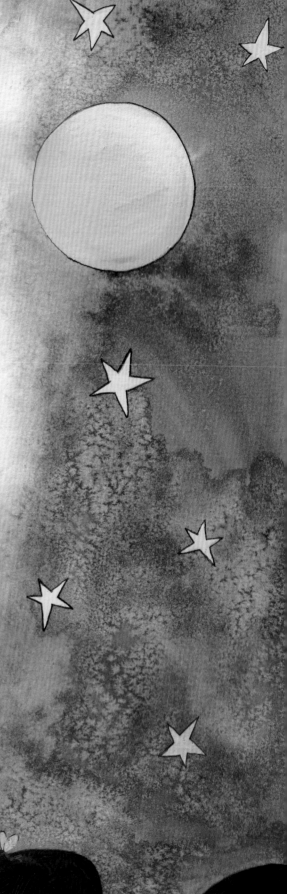

When the World is Dark at Night

When the world seems so dark at night,
I sometimes shiver, shake with fright.
The cheerful birds that sing at day,
sound somehow scary when shadows play.

Then suddenly a star I see,
with friends all shining down on me,
and though the sun has slid from sight,
the moon, a mirror, reflects her light.

Crickets commence concerts of song.
The fire-flies dance, flicker along.
Such merriment upon the lawn,
my foolish fears of the night are gone.

We'll waste our time being afraid,
of wonderful things God has made,
until we learn to look for light,
and find it shining both day and night.

Wee Willie Wheezer Wharnsby

Willie Wheezer Wharnsby,
once wanted to miss school.
He thought up quite a lie,
his mother for to fool.
"I'm sick", he said in bed,
"I think I've caught the flu!
My eyes are seeing polka-dots!
My tongue is turning blue!"

"Oh Willie Wheezer son,"
young Willie's mother said,
"I've seen that blue gum wad
you spat out 'neath the bed.
You can't fool me my boy,
for I've caught you instead.
So get your blue tongue off to school,
before I'm seeing red!"

Well, later that same day
the strangest thing occurred,
Willie Wheezer Wharnsby's,
eyesight became all blurred!
His skin turned kinda green,
temperature rose some.
He felt so really not-so-good,
the school nurse called his mum.

Willie Wheezer's mother,
was not at all amused.
Willie Wheezer's school nurse,
was wildly confused.
Wee Willie's mother's trust,
he sadly had abused.
When asked if they could send him home,
Wee Willie's mum refused.

The moral of the story,
as you, I'm sure, can see,
is not to tell falsehoods,
like Wee Willie Wharnsby.
Most folks trust in the truth,
and truth is: they won't trust
our words made up of lies, and so,
our honesty is a must.

Willie Wheezer Wharnsby,
once wanted to miss school.
He thought up quite a lie,
his mother for to fool.
"I'm sick", he said in bed,
"I think I've caught the flu!
Awww, mum it's just no use there is,
no way I could fool you!"

A Prayer to End Bullying

Here come those other kids,
the worst part of each day.
They act so tough,
and get so rough,
whenever they come my way.

They don't have sticks or stones,
but words and things they say,
hurt just as bad,
leave me so sad,
with scars that won't go away.

I heard a story once,
a prophet long ago,
tried hard to reach,
to give, to teach,
those who didn't want to know.

The people laughed at him,
like those kids laugh my way.
But he stayed strong,
was helped along
by *Allah*, and so I pray –

Allah, help me be strong,
with teachers, parents, friends –
to try my best,
and never rest,
until all bullying ends.

My Mother

I saw my mother's photograph, when she was young like me,
a ponytail, fine flowered frock, and plaster on her knee.
She stood smiling with her own mum, who I call my Granny,
and now I think I understand, this thing called family.

It means we are all connected, like links that make a chain,
like petals on a flower stem, like streams of pouring rain.
Each link like a ring of love, and each leaf one of a kind,
each raindrop different from the rest, no two alike you'll find.

Our lives all intertwine, as we grow, one from the other,
and so with passing time, maybe I will be a mother.
My mum will become a Granny, as on our family grows,
to the beautiful baby buds, who share the same shaped nose!

My Father's Beard

My father has some whiskers,
a beard that's so cuddly,
when he tries to kiss my cheek,
it's always scrubbing me.

He teases and he tickles,
my neck and 'neath my chin.
His beard puts me in giggles,
then loud, long laughs begin!

Within his wispy whiskers,
I've noticed something new,
sprouting between the brown ones,
white hairs are showing through.

He says his beard is changing,
from brown to wintry white,
that each new strand of silver,
is like a bit of light.
He says the more he loves me
the more his love will show,
for as his love gets stronger,
the more white hairs will grow.

My father has some whiskers,
a beard that's so cuddly,
when he tries to kiss my cheek,
it's always scrubbing me.

He teases and he tickles,
my neck and 'neath my chin.
His beard puts me in giggles,
then loud, long laughs begin!

Prayer

I see my parents stand each day,
many times,
turned the same way.
They bow and kneel and sit and then,
up they get
to stand again!

They whisper words so sweet and low.
What they mean,
I just don't know.
It's such a gentle thing to see,
watching them,
so quietly.

Sometimes I stand just like they do,
move my lips,
fold my hands too.
Or I curl up there on their mat,
at their toes,
just like a cat.
And if I try to speak a word,
it's as if,
they never heard.
Then when their done they turn to me,
smile and lift
me on their knee.

They call these times, their times for prayer.
Thanking God,
for all we share.
I've never seen God's face or hand,
but somehow,
I understand.

The cozy feeling that I feel,
helps me know,
that God is real.
Oh how I love these times each day,
when we all,
thank God and pray.

Little Baby

Little Baby,
you cry and coo.
You gurgle and you giggle,
your life is so new.
I've been patient,
waiting for you,
so we could have some fun but,
sleep is all you do!

Little Baby,
along you came.
I helped to choose your first toy,
helped to choose your name.
Mum and Daddy,
would always say,
I was their little baby,
then you came to stay.

I was worried,
yes it is true,
that they would stop loving me,
to start loving you.
Little Baby,
I was so wrong.
The love got even stronger,
since you came along.

Little Baby,
now as you grow,
as you learn to talk and walk,
one thing you should know.
That family,
is like a pot.
The more you put inside it,
the more soup you got!

Little Baby,
you burp and poo.
You wobble and you wiggle,
your life is so new.
Little Baby,
well since you came,
I discovered Mum and Dad,
love us both the same!

Simple Life

There's always work that must be done,
must be done! Everyone!
Life's so simple when we simply
work to make it fun.

Mama's going to fetch the milk,
fetch the milk, fetch the milk
mama's going to fetch the milk
she's gone to get the cow.

Popa's going to plant some corn,
plant some corn, plant some corn.
Popa's going to plant some corn,
he's gone to fetch the plough.

There's always work that must be done,
must be done! Everyone!
Life's so simple when we simply
work to make it fun.

Brother's going to bring the bread,
bring the bread, bring the bread,
brother's going to bring the bread
He's gone to knead the dough.

Grandpa gets honey from the bees
from the bees, from the bees.
He's so brave to be by the,
bee hives all in a row.

There's always work that must be done,
must be done! Everyone!
Life's so simple when we simply
work to make it fun.

Grandmother clucks, "Collect the eggs!
Get the eggs! Get the eggs!"
But I forget to get the eggs,
chase chickens 'round the yard.

We love to live a simple life,
simple life, simple life.
We simply love the life we live,
though some may think its hard.

There's always work that must be done,
must be done! Everyone!
Life's so simple when we simply
work to make it fun.

Though some may think its hard.
Chase chickens 'round the yard,
by bee hives in a row,
while brother kneads the dough,
and father gets the plough,
and mother milks the cow.

I had a Chirpy Chick

I had a chirpy chick,
so small, so yellow and sweet.
A fuzzy flapping friend,
with the cutest tiny feet.
She hatched from in an egg,
her shell cracked and out she came.
Each day I played with her,
and each day she looked the same.

Then all at once things changed,
when I left one summer day,
to visit my grandma,
at her house so far away.
My grandma grabbed my cheeks,
cried "How I have missed you so!
You've grown up oh so fast!
Where'd my little baby go?"

Summer passed at Grandma's,
and I traveled home again,
to find my chirpy chick
had grown up into a hen!
At first I was quite shocked,
and a little sad because,
I missed her tiny feet,
and I missed her fuzzy fuzz.

I think I sort of know,
why my Grandma hugs me so,
why there's tears in her eyes,
when its time for me to go.
Perhaps she gets afraid,
if I grow while we're apart,
that all the fun we've had,
won't stay long within my heart.

I'll always love my chick,
with her feathers and strong legs.
Memories of chirping,
come back when she shares fresh eggs.
I'll always love grandma,
no matter how much I grow.
I'll call to share that more,
so she'll always, always know.

Piles of Smiles

Somewhere there is a room,
where there is no grey or gloom.
The place is full of light, with teeth all gleaming white,
and there are piles of smiles on the ground.

Someone misplaced the key,
causing global tragedy.
Somehow, the door, it seems, pinched closed on people's dreams,
and hid piles of smiles, yet to be found.

Someday we'll realize,
perhaps, much to our surprise,
keys to free a smile, have been with us all the while.
Look for good, and spread that good around.

All the smiles we set free,
will get stuck on you and me,
be gifts of charity,
to share so easily,
Oh – all the piles of smiles will astound!

Someday we'll see a place,
where upon each person's face,
there'll be a smile sign,
that everybody's fine,
and there'll be piles of smiles all around!

There will be piles of smiles on the ground!
Oh – all the piles of smiles will astound!
Yes there'll be piles of smiles all around!

The Ant

Oh little ant,
    I watch you below,
    I watch where you run,
    I watch where you go.

Oh little ant,
    you carry a snack,
    as big as yourself,
    up there on your back.

Oh little ant,
    you do struggle long,
    with a boulder crumb,
    but your faith so strong.

Oh little ant,
    I learn from your way,
    to try, though it's hard,
    being strong each day.

Oh little ant,
    we're really both small.
    As I watch you,
    Allah's above us all.

Busy Buzzing Bees

A busy buzzing bee, is a lot like me,
It works and it lives in community.

From tower to tower it floats by the hour,
guided by God to blooms on each flower.

Sipping nectar sweet, pollen stuck to it's feet,
Helping to spread spring as it stops to eat.

Then back to it's home, to the hive, to the comb,
to jig for it's friends of where it did roam.

Then, in their colony, each small busy bee,
turns nectar they've brought to sweet smooth honey.

We both work hard, buzz busily in the yard.
Have houses we build, loved ones that we guard.

We have skills to respect and gifts to protect.
What we give, can heal – for those who reflect.

A busy buzzing bee! A wonder to see!
Our lives much the same in community!

The Fly, The Spider and I

So smart and strong, from my head to my feet!
Feast fit for a king, I'll sit to eat!
A cheeky fly lands thereupon,
to steal his meal and then fly on.

Spider spin a web! Such a sight to see!
The frailest house that ever could be.
But if that fly gets caught therein,
he never will get out again.

Everything God has made, upon the earth,
has a time, a purpose and a worth.
All things must change, flow, come and go,
as spider, fly and I now know.

Corn

Have you seen stocks of corn, all growing in a field?
How many by the mile, how many cobs they yield.
And upon every cob, so many kernels grow,
so small – side by side – row upon row upon row.

You would get so weary, your eyes would start to strain,
trying to take count of each tiny golden grain.
Add them on your fingers, right down to your last toe,
try to find their number, but you could never know.

Imagine if each grain, was planted yet again,
how many stalks would sprout! A million more plus ten!
They could end all hunger and hope could then take seed!
Imagine if each grain, was really a good deed?

Each pleasing thing we do, each kind word that we say,
to people all around us, at home, work and play.
They're all like little seeds, they grow and grow and grow.
Small but side by side, row upon row upon row.

Hug the World

So much that's new!
Such things to do!
There's life to live,
and love to give!
Let go and hug the world!

So much to know,
'bout how to grow!
Let the world see,
the best of me!
Let go and hug the world!

So much to try!
I wonder why,
some people don't,
some people won't,
let go and hug the world.

Let's hug the world.
Let's go and hug the world!

My Name is Nimboo

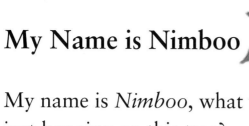

My name is *Nimboo*, what will I do,
just hanging on this tree?
I sigh a lemon sigh, just wondering why,
nobody is picking me?

The last picking day, I heard them say,
they wanted something sweet,
and they passed me – oh dear, so high way up here,
saying "He's too sour to eat!".

But who's to say? Tell me, who are they,
to think I'm just not good?
God made me yellow, a tart little fellow,
I'd remind them if I could!

There's plenty of use, for lemon juice,
Though it makes lips a-pucker.
A little lemon tart, is quite a fine art,
who'd not love a lemon sucker?

Oh – What's that now? Who's quaking my bough?
A hand reaching my way.
Of all of the rest, it thinks I am the best,
and will take me home today.

Now I may be, a warm lemon tea,
maybe marmalade jam!
Such a wonderful treat, this person so sweet,
loves me just for what I am.

Candy People

People are a lot like candy!
There're all so different and dandy.
The way they look and what they do.
Which sweet am I? Which treat are you?

Skin like honey or milky fair,
or coco brown with chocolate hair.
Custard yellow or molasses dark,
or rusty dust of cinnamon bark!

Some friends stick around like toffee,
they're lasting and silly and strong.
Some friends are more like chewing gum:
their fun and flavour won't stay long.

Lean like licorice or lollypop round,
all shapes and colours by the pound.
Small hazelnut or almond eyes,
our wrappers disguise such surprise.

Some candy people that you meet,
are mushy and gooey and sweet.
Some come from life's jawbreaker bin,
but time will melt to mint within.

People are a lot like candy!
Bonbons so different and dandy.
Step to the window, gaze and stop,
at God's great goodie sugar shop.

People are a lot like candy!
There're all so different and dandy.
The way they look and what they do.
Which sweet am I? Which treat are you?

Dear Mr. Crow

Dear Mister Crow,
what makes you laugh?
Way up there in that tree?
With your "Caw, caw, caw!"
Crackled "Ha, ha, ha!"
What is it that you see?

Dear little one,
people – caw, caw –
I watch so far below,
thinking their more free,
than a bird like me,
flying each place I go.

Fences and forts,
with walls and flags,
caw, caw – they're so funny!
The foolish big boys,
who fight with their toys.
are so sadly silly!

Dear Little child,
I'll tell you now,
caw, caw – it's just my view,
this world is so vast,
but won't ever last,
'till changed by those like you.

The Mosque

Now tell me, have you ever heard of a mosque before?
Have you ever seen one? Have you stepped inside its door?

It's a place where people gather, many times a day.
A place to read and learn and a place to stop and pray.

Mosques have been important throughout years and centuries.
Places for good faithful folks to build communities.

Sometimes they may house schools, doctors helping others heal,
or kitchens feeding people who struggle for a meal.

At festivals and weddings, they're bright with songs and cheers.
At times of loss or sadness, they're washed with people's tears.

Mosques are on the earth in almost each land you can name,
London, Beijing, Timbuktu - they never look the same.

Some are made with domes and towers, gold and marble halls.
Some are made of mud and grass. Some have no roof or walls!

But you must go in a mosque to see its treasure there.
The wealth of different people, gathering for prayer.
'Cause for all the gold and riches, minarets as well,
if a mosque sits life-less, it is just a wasted shell.

The heart of every mosque, beats within a *Muslim*'s chest.
That's the thing about a mosque, I really think is best.

So if you have no building called a mosque in your town,
well, you can make your own, simply just by bowing down.

Where you rest your head, just set your mind and place your heart,
that will be the special spot for a new mosque to start.

All of Us

All of us, ride in the same bus.
Shop at the same malls and stores.
All of us, debate and discuss,
decide and divide what is mine and what's yours.

But when it rains,
it rains on all our houses.
We all get cold when it snows.
And when a storm rolls in,
huddled up against our windows,
we all feel the fear when a strong wind blows,
'cause on this earth, we're all of equal worth.

You and I, wonder at the sky,
call God a different name.
As we try – learn and long to fly.
You and I are so differently the same.

We squint our eyes,
when sun shines on the water.
Swim the way a river flows.
As we all get older,
and pricked by thorns to smell life's rose,
we all feel sad when someone we love goes,
'cause on this earth, we're all of equal worth.

As we try – learn and long to fly,
while on this earth, we're all of equal worth.

Alhamdulillah, Subhanallah and Insha Allah

There was a bird,
there was a tree.
There was a flower,
there was a bee.
I thanked God for all that I saw
and I sang out, *alhamdulillah*.

There was a house,
made out of sticks.
There was a city,
made out of bricks.
I was amazed at what I saw,
All I could say was, *subhanallah*.

I saw a dream,
Earth – safe and green.
No hunger, no war.
Water so clean.
I'll work for the world that I saw,
set my mind and say *insha Allah*.

Peep Hole on the World

There's a peep hole looking out, of the front door of my house,
when I push my eye up to it I can see out to the street.
I spy people walking by,
but from the outside passing me,
just a plain front door is all those passing people see.

It seems to me, God has a special peep hole on the world,
and is aware of all we do as we go about our day.
When we're kind and when we smile,
When we fight and when we fuss,
Though we can't see God we can't forget that God sees us.

Daily Prayers

Birds in the trees, sing sweet melodies,
in the morning they whistle and tweet.
First light of day they call me to pray,
as I snuggle beneath my bed sheet.

As day goes by, the sun up so high,
whispers down to the world far below.
"Get off the street and out of the heat,
thanking God for your day as you go."

Our shadows run, and though it's such fun,
chasing them with the time everywhere,
they bow and they grow, letting us know,
that it's time to come join them in prayer.

The sun will sink and you may well think,
that your playtime has slid by too fast.
Ease your fears as the white moon appears,
ask God to let fun memories last.

When the night skies, bring sleep to your eyes,
take a moment to lower your head,
thank God again, for your day – and then,
snuggle back to your dreams and your bed.

Ramadan is on it's Way

Ramadan! *Ramadan*!
Ramadan is on its way!
I'll fast with my whole family.
Can't wait for the first day.
We'll wake up before the sun,
we'll eat and drink and pray,
then fast just as *Allah* has asked.
Ramadan is on it's way.

Ramadan! *Ramadan*!
I've been waiting oh so long,
for you to come and test me out,
see how I've grown so strong.
I'll show you how kind I am,
to every one I meet.
I'll fast just as *Allah* has asked.
There's no food could be as sweet!

Muhammad?

Allah gave the *Qur'an*,
to a very special man,
who passed it on to us,
for the rest of all our days.
Though it was long ago,
his good name, I know you'll know,
was, of course, Muhammad,
upon him, be peace, always.

Of all the things we're told,
of the ancient times of old,
the myths and legends grow,
to things fantasy's made of.
You ask me, "Was he real?"
Did he walk and did he feel?
This prophet of *Allah*?
This man we are taught to love."

The proof is very clear,
in the gifts he left us here,
The wisdom of *Qur'an*
and example of his ways.
They're like a shining light,
that will guide toward what's right,
now passed along to us,
for the rest of all our days.

Dear God

Dear God – I've heard Your Name, from teachers, family
and friends.
You made the universe, and so will live on when it ends.

But everyone I know admits, they've never seen Your Face,
they are not sure where You live and have no map to the place.

I thought perhaps a letter or a postcard could be mailed,
since I didn't have Your address that idea kinda failed.

My Mum told me that I can talk to You if I just pray,
so God – well – here I am, though I'm not sure just what to say.

She said I'd never see You, but she said You're always there,
You're never fast asleep and somehow You're always aware.

She said that You'd remember me, if I remember You,
said You'd always help me if I ever asked You to.

I am just one child You made, out of millions I would guess,
I try my best but sometimes even that turns out a mess.

So I'd like You to help me with the stuff that I find tough –
like feeling sad and lonely or like I'm not good enough.

I'd gladly pay the debt somehow, give something back to You,
but since You're Lord of everything, there's not much I could do.

The only things that come to mind, to make this all seem fair,
are to thank You and remember that You are always there.

Glossary

Alhamdulillah – 'All praise is to God.' (Arabic)

Allah – 'The God'. (Arabic)

Bismillah – 'In the name of the God'. (Arabic)

Insha Allah – 'God willing.' (Arabic)

Muslim – One who is engaged in acts of 'willful surrender' or 'willful submission' to God; the action of 'entering into peace'. The Arabic word *Muslim* stems from the root letters *s-l-m* (*salam*), meaning 'peace'. (Arabic)

Nimboo – 'Lemon.' (Urdu)

Qur'an – '(The) Recitation' or 'That which is to be recited', in reference to the collected recitations of Muhammad, upon whom be peace, described within as being a revelation from God. (Arabic)

Ramadan – The ninth month of the lunar calendar. The Qur'an decrees this a 'sacred month' to be a period of worship and fasting for believers. (Arabic)

Subhanallah – 'Glory be to God.' (Arabic)

About the Author

Dawud Wharnsby was born in Canada in 1972. He has been writing stories, songs and poems for people of all ages for many years. When he is not traveling to sing with audiences around the world, he loves being with his family — hiking in the mountains near his home, growing vegetables and fixing things that get broken around the house. Dawud loves adventures and being outdoors so much that he is an official Ambassador for Scouting (UK), encouraging young people to take care of the earth and build strong communities. The Wharnsby family lives seasonally between their homes in Pakistan, Canada and the United States.